The Headlands

by Christopher Chen

FOR PRODUCTION INQUIRIES

UNITED STATES AND CANADA
info@concordtheatricals.com
1-866-979-0447

UNITED KINGDOM AND EUROPE
licensing@concordtheatricals.co.uk
020-7054-7200

Each title is subject to availability from Concord Theatricals Corp., depending upon country of performance. Please be aware that *THE HEADLANDS* may not be licensed by Concord Theatricals Corp. in your territory. Professional and amateur producers should contact the nearest Concord Theatricals Corp. office or licensing partner to verify availability.

No one shall make any changes in this title(s) for the purpose of production. No part of this book may be reproduced, stored in a retrieval system, scanned, uploaded, or transmitted in any form, by any means, now known or yet to be invented, including mechanical, electronic, digital, photocopying, recording, videotaping, or otherwise, without the prior written permission of the publisher. No one shall share this title(s), or any part of this title(s), through any social media or file hosting websites.

For all inquiries regarding motion picture, television, online/digital and other media rights, please contact Concord Theatricals Corp.

MUSIC AND THIRD-PARTY MATERIALS USE NOTE

Licensees are solely responsible for obtaining formal written permission from copyright owners to use copyrighted music and/or other copyrighted third-party materials (e.g., artworks, logos) in the performance of this play and are strongly cautioned to do so. If no such permission is obtained by the licensee, then the licensee must use only original music and materials that the licensee owns and controls. Licensees are solely responsible and liable for clearances of all third-party copyrighted materials, including without limitation music, and shall indemnify the copyright owners of the play(s) and their licensing agent, Concord Theatricals Corp., against any costs, expenses, losses and liabilities arising from the use of such copyrighted third-party materials by licensees. For music, please contact the appropriate music licensing authority in your territory for the rights to any incidental music.

IMPORTANT BILLING AND CREDIT REQUIREMENTS

If you have obtained performance rights to this title, please refer to your licensing agreement for important billing and credit requirements.

THE HEADLANDS was first produced by LCT3/Lincoln Center Theater, in New York, New York on February 8, 2020. The performance was directed by Knud Adams, with sets by Kimie Nishikawa, costumes by Tilly Grimes, lights by Mark Barton, sound by Peter Mills Weiss, and projections by Ruey Horng Sun. The production stage manager was Joshua Mark Gustafson. The cast was as follows:

HENRY..Aaron Yoo
GEORGE...Johnny Wu
LEENA..Laura Kai Chen
JESS...Mahira Kakkar
PAT / LEENA (OLDER).............................Mia Katigbak
WALTER / DETECTIVE..............................Henry Stram
TOM...Edward Chin-Lyn

CHARACTERS

HENRY – Chinese-American, male, thirties.

GEORGE – Chinese, male, twenties and forties.

LEENA – Chinese-American, female, twenties, forties.

JESS – Female, thirties.

PAT / LEENA (OLDER) – Chinese female, seventies.

WALTER / DETECTIVE – Imagined as male, at least fifties.

TOM – Chinese-American, male, twenties and forties.

AUTHOR'S NOTES

The roles of Pat / Leena (older) and Walter / Detective are lumped together for easy casting, but they can be split apart. POC casting encouraged for Jess.

A slash (" / ") means overlapping dialogue.

VIDEO

This play ultimately takes place inside of the mind. A series of large projection surfaces are the primary features of the set, with a very minimalist playing area in front. The purpose of video is to create an all-encompassing, ever-shifting neural landscape as we quickly jump from place to place in memories and filaments of the subconscious, with different layers of the mind reflected simultaneously. I've expressed the character of the video in the script as this...

...with each block representing a different video surface. Please note that this grid, and the elements I put inside them are *only suggestions* that point to how video should function scene by scene throughout the play. In practice, a director, set designer and video designer can and should go beyond this, using their own discretion as to what goes in each video at any given moment, and even how many surfaces there should be. Six is arbitrary. The size and shape of surfaces can also vary, and in sum they should give the impression of a complex system that is a composite of many fragments (the brain being a composite of disparate memory fragments). It is strongly preferable that this concept be embodied by many different, discrete physical projection surfaces, each surface dedicated to a single image at a time; as opposed to, say, one or two giant single screens with many different image areas within. Above all, the main directive is that video must be always present and all-encompassing.

NOTE: Licensees must acquire rights for any copyrighted images. One suggested piece of video content is *Batman: The Animated Series*, which is copyrighted. If the licensee wants to go this route, they must create images that suggest the series, but do not infringe on the copyright.

TONE

Inspired by *Vertigo* and other San Francisco noir, as well as the exquisitely precise tone management of Kazuo Ishiguro's novels, the play's primary requirement for its creative team will be to make each scene, each moment, a highly distinct pocket of atmosphere, mood and emotion. There should be a cinematic quality to each scene, and to the flow of the production as a whole.

INTRODUCTION

*(**HENRY** onstage, looking at a blank screen. He holds this for a beat, then he turns to the audience.)*

HENRY. There are so many ways to make an introduction. And I'm not sure what the *best* way is, so I'm just gonna jump right in. Okay?

Hi, my name is Henry. And because you *must* be defined by your job, I'll start by saying I'm an engineer at Google, aaand enough about that. I also have a serious girlfriend, I'm a big time film buff – film noir – and... I have a side hobby. That's what I really want to talk to you about.

On the side, I'm an amateur sleuth. What this means is I do independent research on cold cases, on my own, just for kicks. Long before *Serial, Making a Murderer, I* was a true crime aficionado, before it became cool.

Tonight I'm going to tell you about one particular case I studied. An unsolved case that's stuck with me for a long time. It's a murder, so buckle up. I'll walk you through the details.

Ready for this?

The victim is George Wong, a kitchen contractor who lived in the Sunset District of San Francisco.

*(One panel of screen area comes alive for the first time. We see **GEORGE** onscreen. On another screen or two we see pictures of the Sunset District.)*

George	Blank	Sunset District
Blank	Sunset District	Blank

He was shot in his own home. Right in the living room. Single bullet to the side of the head.

George	Crime scene image	Sunset District
Crime scene image	His home from the outside	Crime scene image

The official story? It's a burglary gone wrong. Computers and jewelry are stolen, the place is torn up.

George	Crime scene image	Crime scene image
Crime scene image	Crime scene image	Crime scene image

It's the middle of the day, so Mr. Wong shouldn't be home. For some reason he is, he surprises the burglar, burglar has a gun and shoots him, runs away. This is the official story, and it rings true because there had been several unsolved burglaries in the neighborhood within the last few months. The only person they briefly look into is a Paul Cheung, employee of Mr. Wong's who has a criminal history. He's cleared once his alibi checks out. Now, why is he even suspected? For a brief moment there's a theory that the home invasion part was staged, and the killer is someone Mr. Wong knew. What makes them think this? The question of... How did the intruder get in.

George		Front door	Front door detail
Crime scene image		Garage	Front door from afar

In other burglaries in the neighborhood, the robbers used coat hangers to trigger garage doors open. Not the case here. Front door is simply unlocked, and the garage door is locked, no signs of forced entry. So maybe

Mr. Wong simply forgot to lock the door? Or maybe... he let them in himself? A delivery man in disguise? Who knows. But doesn't fit the burglary pattern.

George	Blank	Blank
Blank	Blank	Blank

As for witnesses, there aren't any. Neighbors are questioned, some *think* they heard the gunshot, but assumed it was a car backfiring. Time of death is placed at around twelve noonish, and Mr. Wong was found at 4:21 p.m. when his wife, Leena Wong, returned home. His wife has an alibi too. Mrs. Wong...

(We see **LEENA** *onscreen.)*

George	Blank	Leena
Blank	Blank	Blank

...was a piano teacher at the San Francisco Conservatory of music. She was with a student at the time and came home right after. Their son was at his friend Martin's house – they often took him after school – and thankfully wasn't with his mother when she made the grim discovery.

By all accounts they were a very loving and happy family. But were they really? Was everything *really* okay? This is the thread I started to pull. While the physical trail went cold, there may have been more in the *personal* realm than previously known. Let's take a look.

The Dinner Table

Kitchen wall	Window showing nighttime outside	Kitchen wall
Blank	Blank	Blank

*(The dinner table. **GEORGE** is sitting there, silently. **LEENA** is standing nearby, paused in the middle of an activity. Charged tension. **GEORGE** doesn't react.)*

LEENA. I just wish uh...

GEORGE. There was something more you could do.

*(He waits while **LEENA** somehow indicates the affirmative.)*

LEENA. I want us to be a team on this. Like always.

*(**GEORGE** doesn't respond.)*

You're just...acting very different now.

GEORGE. I'm sorry.

LEENA. It's just...very hard.

*(They stop suddenly, look out into the audience – or **HENRY**. The play sits in a slightly awkward beat.)*

HENRY. Okay so I know this doesn't make a lot of sense out of context. But this, along with many other instances, will add up. They're clues.

They had this strange conversation in the kitchen about a week before he died. They stop when they see me in the doorway. Oh, I'm their son. Sorry for not telling you earlier, just wanted to – get the facts out there first. Felt easier to remove myself.

Anyway, he died about two decades ago. I was ten. And when I think back to that time, other memories start to return.

Maybe *they*...are the missing evidence.

Hospital

Hospital imagery	Hospital imagery	Hospital imagery
Leena behind scrim?	Hospital imagery	EKG machine

(**HENRY** *by* **LEENA (OLDER)***'s side.*)

HENRY. But first: how did I come to think there was more to the case than the official story? Well, it's as cliched as a deathbed confessional because, well, it's a deathbed confessional. Of sorts. My mother was struck with cancer in her seventies, and in her morphine delirium, she'd sometimes say things that didn't make a lot of sense.

LEENA (OLDER). George...

HENRY. This is Henry.

LEENA (OLDER). Don't confuse me.

> (**HENRY** *doesn't respond. Goes and holds her hand.*)

HENRY. Are you remembering Dad?

LEENA (OLDER). Of course I remember him.

> (*Beat.*)

There's too much...despair.

> (**HENRY** *nods solemnly.*)

He wasn't happy.

HENRY. (*Suddenly interested.*) Wait – what do you mean? He seemed pretty happy to me.

> (**LEENA** *shakes her head.*)

LEENA (OLDER). I'm talking about his death, his death.

HENRY. What about it?

LEENA (OLDER). His death. He was in despair. I tried to help him.

> *(Slight beat.)*

HENRY. What do you mean by that? Help him? How? His death was...

> **(LEENA (OLDER)** *suddenly snaps out of it.)*

LEENA (OLDER). Oh, you know what happened. It was a burglary.

HENRY. Wait, but you just said...

LEENA (OLDER). Please. I don't want to talk about this. I need to sleep.

HENRY. *(To audience.)* Of course, she never mentioned this again. And she passed away soon after. But what did she mean...

> *(As he says the following, the text types out onscreen...)*

"I'm talking about his death. He was in despair. I tried to help him."

...his death.	He was in	despair.
I tried	to help him	.

Despair? So...suicide? *My father?* Inconceivable. And yet, going back to my memories...

The Window

Aspects of living room	Living room window, blinds open	Aspects of living room
Aspects of living room	Closer view of the night street	Aspects of living room

(**GEORGE** *standing still, looking out a window.*)

HENRY. It's near the time of his death and he's looking out the window. Just staring. At the time I thought this is just something adults do, but now I know adults don't have time to stand around and stare blankly at things; and we lived in the sleepy, fog-banked Sunset District, where there wouldn't be much to look at anyway. I come to the window too, don't see anything of note, so I ask: (*To* **GEORGE**.) What are you looking at?

GEORGE. Nothing. Just thinking.

HENRY. Why are you looking out the window?

GEORGE. (*Looking out.*) It's nice sometimes to look out and not in.

(*He looks at* **HENRY**.)

(*Smiling.*) Or you can get trapped in your own brain. Do you know what I mean by that?

HENRY. Uhh…

GEORGE. Your dad's just being weird.

HENRY. (*To audience.*) No shit.

(*He looks at* **GEORGE** *at the window again. The melancholy has returned. They hold this pose for a beat.*)

I'd forgotten about this episode, but looking back on it now, its strangeness, I see it as the clue it is.

Piano

HENRY.   Here's another instance. My mother was the pianist, but my father liked to plunk around on the keys. And in the days before his death, he started exclusively playing these chords, improvised by him.

(**GEORGE** *sits down, as if before a keyboard. We hear the music.*)

George's left hand on keyboard	George's eyes	George's right hand at keyboard
The living room window from before	The street view from the window from before	An element of the crime scene

I didn't think much of his playing at the time, but thinking back I can identify an obsessiveness to it, like that same faraway trance I saw at the window. Why is he playing these chords? With the help of a musician friend I was able to pick them out. My friend said the chords were primarily suspended chords. So, you have the tonic, the harmonious chords, and then you have suspended chords where one note is off, suspended. The note *wants* to resolve, but never quite reaches it.

Animation demonstrating suspended chords, using the music, across multiple screens
Both of George's hands playing the music on keyboard.

A stretch, right? To think that unresolved, *searching* chords somehow reflect the hidden pathos of a man? But again, this is unusual behavior, and he's playing these odd chords a week before he dies.

Hiking with Father

HENRY. I need to emphasize here that my father was not usually a melancholy man. My mother was very happy too, I had a pretty loving and idyllic childhood. They took me on a lot of adventures...

> *(Images of different places in San Francisco cycle through the video screens underneath the following as they are described. Some are noted below, but they should always be in motion. Nostalgic music should accompany, something of the feel of Satie's "Gymnopedie No. 1.")*

San Francisco playgrounds with sports. Old photos of father and son?	San Francisco museums	Ghiradelli Square and Golden Gate Bridge
Mission District burritos and murals	Golden Gate Park and Ocean Beach. Old photos of them?	House fun – toys, backyards etc. Old photos of them?

I remember playgrounds, friends, the beach, all kinds of museums. I remember San Francisco so vividly: the bustling Mission District, the wild foliage of Golden Gate Park. They'd take me everywhere, and when you're a kid following your parents, these places you travel to feel like extensions of your home, do you know what I mean? They imprint in your mind the sense of *place* being connected to...*safety*. I especially cherished memories of places my father took me one on one.

---

* A license to produce *The Headlands* does not include a performance license for any third-party or copyrighted music. Licensees should create an original composition or use music in the public domain. For further information, please see the Music and Third Party Materials Use Note on page iii.

(The below noted images/video should change in a staggered manner as they are described.)

Marin Headlands from a distance	Images of Lucca's Delicatessen	Video of crossing the Golden Gate Bridge
On the Marin Headlands path	The spot with the view	The view of San Francisco/ Land's End

There was one place that seemed to have particular importance to him: a hike in the Marin Headlands, right outside the city across the Golden Gate Bridge. It became a ritual for us, one that seemed very deliberately choreographed. It always started with a trip to Lucca's Delicatessen in The Marina for sandwiches. The first time I wanted turkey. He said:

GEORGE. Get the Italian Combo.

HENRY. I want turkey.

GEORGE. Trust me.

(Images of the Golden Gate Bridge drive onscreen.)

HENRY. After numerous trips I had to admit he was right, and the Italian Combo became the most treasured part of the ritual. Then comes the hike. Again, deliberately planned. The first time I said...

(Images of the hike onscreen.)

*(To **GEORGE**.)* I want to stop here. Let's eat here.

GEORGE. No. There's a special spot up further.

HENRY. I'm hungry now.

GEORGE. Just a little further.

HENRY. We get to the spot. It's the view that he wants.

(Images of San Francisco from afar.)

GEORGE. You see that! Doesn't the city look amazing from here?

HENRY. Yeah.

GEORGE. And you see, that area right over there...those trees on those cliffs. Do you see it?

HENRY. Uh huh.

GEORGE. That's where I first met your mother.

HENRY. On the cliffs?

GEORGE. Yep! We were sitting on the cliffside, on the edge of that big, amazing city, looking out...over to here! To where *we* are now!

HENRY. Can we go there?

GEORGE. Sure. But I actually like looking at it from here, from far away.

HENRY. How come?

GEORGE. Because it's a special place, but it's changed. It's much busier now, with tourists all over, taking pictures. Back in the day you could really just sit there and make it your own.

HENRY. He's trying to craft a moment for me. But I can't figure out why. He comes alive during these Marin Headlands outings of ours. But in the week before his death, I ask to go one more time.

(*Video out.*)

GEORGE. No.

HENRY. Why not?

GEORGE. It's too far away.

HENRY. I want to go!

GEORGE. (*Unexpectedly firm.*) No. Not there.

(*Charged pause.*)

EMDR

(Suddenly, a light goes back and forth between screens, like a pendulum, with appropriate "whooshing" sound accompaniment.)

Light...moving...	across...screens...	like... pendulum...

HENRY. I'm currently engaged in a therapy technique known as EMDR: Eye Movement Desensitization and Reprocessing. It helped me a lot with my father's death long ago, and I've taken it up again with my mother's passing. It's a technique for overcoming trauma by reliving specific painful memories while...

(His eyes go back and forth, following the light.)

Having your eyes go back and forth, following a light. This taps into the neural network associated with a trauma and rewires it, in order to...

(His eyes go back and forth.)

Remove it from your sense of self as a whole. Reprogram your memories.

(His eyes go back and forth.)

Blank	Blank	Blank
Blank	Blank	Blank

Like the trauma of the day he died. When my mother finally told me what had happened. It was at a police station. I was at a friend's house before that and his mother, Pat, drove me there. I remember my mother, in tears, telling me. I remember the policeman standing behind her, and wondering why he wasn't comforting her when she was so clearly in distress. How that told me the situation was primitive. I remember understanding this was real, he was gone, but nevertheless thinking let's go home and see him just the same. I remember thinking: "these are emotions I can't handle. But he can help me. He'll know what to do." I want my dad to help me deal with his own death. One of the crazy notions that pops into your – heh.

Jess

Cafe or home or park?	Cafe or home or park?	Cafe or home or park?
Cafe or home or park?	Cafe or home or park?	Cafe or home or park?

*(Throughout, **JESS** and **HENRY** are both "into it," engaged in the puzzle-solving.)*

JESS. Okay so the window, the piano, the hike: this drastic change in character, all within...

HENRY. Within the week before he dies.

JESS. Yeah, that's weird.

HENRY. *(To audience.)* This is Jess, my girlfriend.

JESS. And even *if* it's just coincidence, still the question of *why*, what *caused* this / change.

HENRY. Right, exactly, there had to be *some* reason. *(To audience.)* Jess is a true crime aficionado like me. I turned her into one.

JESS. And he was never really moody.

HENRY. I mean sometimes, but not like this. *(To audience.)* We immerse ourselves in my cold cases together. Some of our favorite memories as a couple involve hunching over crime photographs, brainstorming ways a man's head could have been bludgeoned in.

JESS. But okay, then, just to play devil's advocate... Is there the possibility he was *always* more depressive than you remember, but these *particular* things are jumping out because – you know, memories get heightened around traumatic events. Right?

HENRY. This wasn't normal behavior. And I swear I remember thinking that *at the time they occurred* too. Before knowing he was going to die.

JESS. Mm.

HENRY. Kids are perceptive. They can pick up complex emotions.

JESS. They can.

> *(A beat, while they are lost in their respective thoughts.)*

Heh. I remember just *one* raised eyebrow from my mother, and I could piece together this entire *psychological profile* of a situation.

> *(**HENRY** smiles and does a little chuckle of recognition.)*

Like just one raised eyebrow would tell me my dad had *one* too many beers. And then *he'd* do this *slight* little smile that told me that he was...ashamed, but not *really* ashamed.

HENRY. Sorry not sorry.

JESS. Sorry not sorry, yes. There's no more complex emotion than that.

> *(They both laugh. Then they are lost in thought for a bit.)*

(Back to the case.) Okay. But is there a way to get some outside corroboration?

HENRY. For...

JESS. Your memories. Of your father's mood. Like is there someone *else* who knew your father well at the time, who might *also* have seen this change, this weird depression?

HENRY. I think I know just the person. You're so smart.

JESS. Yeah. *(Obviously.)* So this is like the ultimate case right?

HENRY. The case to end all others.

Differing images of George	Differing images of George	Differing images of George
Differing images of George	Differing images of George	Differing images of George

(Looking at the images, studying them.) My father. Why would he be depressed? What would put him in despair? You have an image of someone. But it's a sliver of an image you're seeing, one that's cropped just for you.

Walter

Walter's house, outside	Living room	Details of living room. Photos?
Hovering memory of young Henry and George	Detail of house	Hovering memory of Walter and George, younger?

(As **WALTER** *enters,* **HENRY** *narrates.)*

HENRY. Walter Bingham in some ways knew my father just as well as my mother did. He started a kitchen contracting business with him back in the very beginning, in 1978. He was almost like a brother to him, and uncle to me, though I hardly saw him since my dad died. I went to visit him at his house in the Noe Valley.

(They embrace when they meet.)

WALTER. Henry how are you.

HENRY. I'm okay, thanks.

WALTER. I'm so sorry about your mother.

HENRY. Thanks.

WALTER. And how are you holding up?

HENRY. One day at a time.

WALTER. Yeah, that's how it is.

(He smiles.)

How's your...wife? / Is it?

HENRY. Girlfriend.

WALTER. Ah.

HENRY. She's good. We're good.

WALTER. That's great to hear.

 (Slight awkward beat.)

HENRY. Uh, hey yeah so the reason why I / came to see you...

WALTER. Yeah.

HENRY. I was wondering if I could talk with you about my father.

WALTER. Yes, of course.

HENRY. Since my mother died, I'm just thinking about *him* again too now, / and...

WALTER. Sure, of course.

HENRY. And this might sound like an odd question, but, I've been thinking about his – his death. And I was just uh...wondering – how you'd describe his – ... I guess... mood, his disposition, right before...it happened.

 (WALTER *doesn't immediately respond.)*

If you can remember.

WALTER. Yeah, it's just – it was so long ago.

HENRY. I guess what I want to know is, did he seem...

WALTER. What.

HENRY. I dunno...different?

WALTER. *Different.* Um...

 (Beat.)

HENRY. Did he seem...*depressed*?

WALTER. Your father never really seemed depressed.

 (Slight beat.)

But look. To be honest. At the time, our business was going through some – a bit of a rough patch. Don't know how much / you...

HENRY. I didn't / know, no.

WALTER. Yeah well... He wouldn't have wanted to bother you with that. He really looked out for you.

(**HENRY** *smiles and nods.*)

So his mood – he might have been a little more...under stress...than usual, around that time. I was too.

HENRY. What kind of rough patch? Like sales?

WALTER. Yeah. But again, it was so long ago, I can't – ...

(*Beat.*)

It's tough to think about.

HENRY. What is?

WALTER. That time. Because of what happened to him.

HENRY. Ah.

WALTER. Why do you ask this? If you don't mind my asking.

HENRY. Well, right before she passed, my mother said my father was...in despair, right before he died.

(*A beat.* **WALTER** *shifts uncomfortably, looks down.* **HENRY** *notices.*)

(*To audience.*) That's when I see it. It's in the way he shifts in his seat, then looks down. (*To* **WALTER.**) There's something you're not telling me... Right?

(*A silence, where* **WALTER** *averts his gaze.*)

It's okay. I'm really just after the truth.

WALTER. You have good memories of your father. Don't you?

HENRY. Yes.

WALTER. And he was a good man. That's the bottom line truth.

HENRY. What is it. Tell me.

(A silence while WALTER *looks at him long and hard.)*

WALTER. Okay. Fine. I'll tell you. I...caught your father.

HENRY. Caught??

WALTER. I caught him. He was...taking money from the company.

(Stunned beat while HENRY *takes it in.)*

HENRY. *(To audience.)* I'm not prepared for this. *(To* WALTER.*)* Like...embezzling? He was embezzling money / from the –

WALTER. Yes. From our company.

HENRY. How? Are you sure? How / could this –

WALTER. There was a discretionary fund. I discovered it was much lower than it should have been. Did some digging around a large withdrawal. I confronted your father, he confessed.

HENRY. How much?

WALTER. A substantial sum.

(He's not going to continue. Slight awkward pause.)

HENRY. Why did he do it?

WALTER. Don't know. Maybe it's easy to cross lines when it's your company, that you started from scratch. I can see that. Nevertheless...

HENRY. So what happened next? Was he – going to leave?/ Or...

WALTER. He was going to leave, yes.

 (*Beat.*)

HENRY. And what about the two of you?

WALTER. What about us?

HENRY. Like – personally.

WALTER. We weren't on good terms, no, at the end. It was a really – tough situation.

HENRY. Did he not want to leave? Or – ...

WALTER. It was more than that.

HENRY. You were going to turn him in? My father?

WALTER. I was talking to my lawyer. To see all options. But yes, that's where we were headed.

 (**HENRY** *does a disbelieving laugh.*)

HENRY. But –

WALTER. But what.

HENRY. You couldn't have – ...worked it out amongst yourselves?

WALTER. Look. This is serious business, okay? The company's bigger than just the two of us. If it was discovered that I knew about this and kept quiet, I'd be in trouble too. Okay? *Your father* put us in this situation, so don't you dare imply that I was in any way responsible for what happened to him, okay? If you're thinking he – he was in *despair* or something. I still loved him. I was devastated by happened to him.

 (*Pause.* **HENRY** *doesn't respond.*)

And he didn't do it to himself anyway, right? It was a burglary.

HENRY. I guess I just thought of you guys as family.

WALTER. Families are complicated. Look, I care about you, but...

    (He stands up.)

This is going to have to end now.

    (Extends hand. **HENRY** *doesn't take it.)*

Take care of yourself.

The Dinner Table

(We immediately see the EMDR pendulum start to swing, indicating a re-ordering of a memory. We see the exact same elements of the recurring dinner set-up again on video and onstage.)

Kitchen wall	Window showing nighttime outside	Kitchen wall
Light...moving...	across...screens...	like... pendulum...

LEENA. I just wish uh...

GEORGE. There was something more you could do.

(He waits while **LEENA** *somehow indicates the affirmative.)*

LEENA. But I want you to let me –

GEORGE. No. I don't need you to help me find a lawyer.

LEENA. But I know people!

GEORGE. I don't want your help. I'm not dragging you in further.

LEENA. I want us to be a team on this. Like always.

*(***GEORGE*** doesn't respond.)*

You're just...acting very different now.

GEORGE. I need to fix my own mistake. By *myself.*

(Beat.)

LEENA. It's just...very hard. I still don't know what possessed you to do it.

(**HENRY** *is revealed to have been watching.*)

HENRY. *(Observing the scene, kind of to himself.)* I remember them fighting about a lawyer once. Was that *this* conversation? Might be conflating two different – ... *(To audience, shaking it off.) Anyway.*

Jess

Cafe or home or park?	Cafe or home or park?	Cafe or home or park?
Cafe or home or park?	Cafe or home or park?	Cafe or home or park?

HENRY. So my father's an embezzler. *(Does a disbelieving laugh.)*

JESS. But *why*, why did he do it. That's the question.

HENRY. Yeah.

JESS. Did you guys have money problems? That you knew of?

HENRY. Not that *I* knew of. But maybe.

JESS. Could he have had, like...debts? Like gambling? Or – sorry / for even suggesting that he –

HENRY. No, no, that – that crossed my mind too. But I don't think so. Not him. That's not him.

(A silence.)

What are you thinking?

JESS. Well just that – I mean it would make sense – if he took his own life – it would make sense if it was something, uh...shameful. Or something. Right? And again, sorry, / for –

HENRY. No, it would. But...

JESS. I mean if you have a *family*, the reason would have to be *so* – ...uh *(Searching for word.)* ...

(Silence.)

Honey I'm sorry, should we keep talking about this?

HENRY. Yeah, why not?

JESS. Sure?

HENRY. Yeah it's no problem.

(*Pause.*)

I *had* actually wondered if we had money problems I didn't know about. Because I thought...maybe it was *life insurance.*

JESS. Ahh. /

HENRY. It wasn't, I checked.

JESS. Oh.

HENRY. But see that, *that* would be more in character for him.

JESS. What.

HENRY. Some big sacrifice, some big noble gesture. Especially for my mother. I mean maybe not as extreme / as – (suicide).

JESS. Right.

HENRY. Because yeah, he worshipped her.

JESS. Mm. He'd make a sacrifice.

HENRY. Yeah.

JESS. That *is* more him than gambling.

HENRY. He was a romantic.

(*Slight beat.*)

JESS. But didn't *she* make the first move? Your mother? I remember from when she was telling us how they / met.

HENRY. Yeah, she approached him first yes. Guess it's a pattern for us Wong men, huh.

JESS. Hm?

HENRY. Women approach us first, we fall hard in response.

JESS. *(Half-playfully.)* We went over this! You came to *me* first!

HENRY. *(Playful.)* No, no, / no.

JESS. Yes! At Jamie's! *You* asked if you could get me a drink!

HENRY. That was *after* we talked on the sofa about Google. And *you* / started that.

JESS. We had our drinks *in our hands* on / the sofa.

HENRY. Yeah, drinks from / before.

JESS. We've already been through this.

HENRY. I was sitting on the sofa and you came up to me, and *we had never met*, and you approached me and said: "Jamie tells me you do UX design at Google."

JESS. No, you were *standing* by the sofa, our eyes met, and you said: "Hey I'm getting another drink, want one?" I said okay, and you said: "Stay there, I wanna talk to you." And I was thinking to myself: that was pretty bad-ass. You're saying it didn't happen that way?

HENRY. Well maybe you're right, maybe that's / how it happened.

JESS. Okay fine, you were a little dweeb, / and I coaxed you out of your little techie shell, we'll use that version.

HENRY. No, okay, you're – ... *(He laughs.)* ... No, no, actually I think my memory's a little *(Hand motion that indicates "shaky.")* – ...

(They laugh.)

(To audience.) But my mother did approach my father. That was for sure. He was a recent immigrant from China, and she was second generation San Franciscan.

They met at Land's End, a San Francisco cliff-side overlooking The Bay.

One evening, a few months before her diagnosis, my mother told us the whole story.

George and Leena

(Images of and from Land's End, looking out over the Bay, including the Golden Gate Bridge. **GEORGE** *is sitting there, with food and a book.* **LEENA (OLDER)** *is talking to* **HENRY** *and* **JESS** *at the table, describing the scene. Nostalgic atmospherics, perhaps reminiscent of the Satie environment from earlier.* **LEENA** *at some point enters under the following monologue and approaches* **GEORGE**.*)*

Views of and from Land's End	Views of and from Land's End	Views of and from Land's End
Views of and from Land's End	Views of and from Land's End	Views of and from Land's End

LEENA (OLDER). I can remember meeting him like it was yesterday. When I saw him sitting there, looking out at the Bay, he looked so content. There was a confidence in him, just sitting there with his lunch and a book, looking out. I wondered what he was doing, but I was first attracted to the food. It smelled like home. Mm. Braised pork, sour cabbage: home cooking you didn't find in restaurants. He must have made it himself. *(To* **GEORGE**.*)* Excuse me, I said.

GEORGE. Yes?

LEENA. Sorry, I was drawn by the smell of your food.

GEORGE. Oh, would you like some?

LEENA. Oh! No, I just wanted to ask – are you Hakka?

GEORGE. I am, yes!

LEENA. My grandmother made a dish exactly like that.

GEORGE. She is...

LEENA. Hakka, yes. She passed away so I haven't smelled those smells in a long time.

GEORGE. Speak Chinese?

LEENA. Poorly.

GEORGE. *(In Chinese. Offering it.)* Smell more. 闻一闻。
(wén yì wén.)

LEENA. *(In Chinese.)* Thank you. 谢谢。
(xiè xiè.)

GEORGE. *(In Chinese.)* Try some. I insist. Here let me find... 尝一下，快尝尝吧，我给你找一个...
(cháng yí xià, kuài cháng cháng ba, wǒ gěi nǐ zhǎo yí gè...)

> *(Fumbles around, trying to find something to serve her with.)*

LEENA. *(In English.)* Oh, well, I can just use yours.

> *(She quickly takes his fork and takes a bite.* **GEORGE** *is taken aback.)*

(In Chinese.) Sorry, I'm so sorry, I don't know what came over me, I – 不好意思，实在对不起，我也不知道刚刚我怎么，我就...
(bù hǎo yì si, shí zài dùi bù qǐ, wǒ yě bù zhī dào gang gāng wǒ zěn me le, wǒ jiù...)

GEORGE. *(In Chinese.)* No! It's okay! 没事，没关系的。
(méi shì, méi guān xī de.)

LEENA. *(In English.)* Here, uh... *(In Chinese.)* Napkin. 纸巾。
(zhǐ jīn.)

> *(She looks around for a napkin.* **GEORGE** *is about to procure one, but before he can, she's wiped the fork off on her clothes. She hands it back.)*

(*In Chinese.*) Sorry again. 实在对不起。

(shí zài dùi bù qǐ.)

(*In English.*) Don't know what came over me.

> (*He gently pushes her hand – with fork – back to her. He also hands her the bowl.*)

GEORGE. (*In Chinese.*) Have more. Please. 请多吃一点。

(qǐng dūo chī yì diǎn.)

> (*She hesitates for a second, then takes another bite. Slight awkward pause. But then they settle in, getting more comfortable. Sounds of the Bay rise up a bit as they look out to it.*)

(*In Chinese.*) It's so beautiful, right? 这里真的很美，对吗？

(zhè lǐ zhēn de hěn měi, dùi ma?)

LEENA. (*In Chinese.*) This is one of my favorite places. 这是我最喜欢的地方之一

(zhè shì wǒ zùi xǐ huān de dì fāng zhī yī.)

GEORGE. (*In Chinese.*) Almost seems...fake. Does that make sense... 这里几乎像是... 假的一样。你明白我的意思吗？

(zhè lǐ hū xiàng shì...jiǎ de yí yàng. nǐ míng bái wǒ de yì sī ma?)

LEENA. (*In Chinese.*) Sure. 当然。

(dāng rán.)

GEORGE. (*In Chinese.*) Like a...you send them... 就好像... 那个你用来寄送的...

(jiù hǎo xiàng...nà gè nǐ yòng lái jì sòng de...)

LEENA. (*In English.*) A postcard.

GEORGE. (*In Chinese.*) Yes. 对的。

(dùi de.)

(*In English.*) Like a postcard.

(Beat.)

JESS. What happened next?

(The same "nostalgic music" as in the hiking scene (reminiscent of Satie).)*

LEENA (OLDER). It was a whirlwind. He was a *true* romantic. He took me all over the city.

Romantic images of S.F. Some with them, younger?	Romantic images of S.F. Some with them, younger?	Romantic images of S.F. Some with them, younger?
Romantic images of S.F. Some with them, younger?	Romantic images of S.F. Some with them, younger?	Romantic images of S.F. Some with them, younger?

Even though I was born and raised here, he made me see it anew. North Beach was a favorite of ours.

North Beach	North Beach	North Beach
North Beach	North Beach	North Beach

GEORGE. Being in a new country, it is like I get to be an outsider crashing a party.

LEENA. You'll have to settle down at some point.

GEORGE. Says who.

LEENA. What if you meet someone who wants to settle down?

GEORGE. The time comes when the person comes.

LEENA. Well okay then.

GEORGE. What I love about a new city is... I get to be more... *(In Chinese.)* awake? 醒过来？

---

*A license to produce *The Headlands* does not include a performance license for any third-party or copyrighted music. Licensees should create an original composition or use music in the public domain. For further information, please see the Music and Third Party Materials Use Note on page iii.

(xǐng gùo lái?)

(In English.) To its – its *(In Chinese.)* details. 细节。
(xì jié.)

(In English.) And magic.

LEENA. Well, I've lived here all my life and it's still magic to me. I want to take you to one of my favorite places.

Coit Tower?	Coit Tower?	Coit Tower?
Coit Tower?	Coit Tower?	Coit Tower?

HENRY. My father of course was smitten. My mother was too, but by society's measures, she was the catch. They were the Chinese-American elite, she was heiress to a shipping fortune, living in a mansion in Pac Heights. My father was a dishwasher living in Chinatown. He tried to play down his insecurities, but...

GEORGE. *(To* **LEENA.***)* I don't know what you see in me.

LEENA (OLDER). *(To* **HENRY** *and* **JESS.***)* He kept saying this throughout our marriage. Got old.

(They are sitting side by side. He kisses her.)

LEENA. That was bold.

(She kisses him back.)

HENRY. My father brought me here *(Indicating screen.)* and told me this was the place where they first kissed. I'm sure they made more memories in his Chinatown apartment too.

Tenement house exterior	The street	Tenement house exterior
Inside hallway	The room	The room

(Quick shots of body parts and skin, indicating sex. They are flickering and go out quickly.)

Close-ups of aspects of the room from their different points of view	Close-ups of aspects of the room from their different points of view	Close-ups of aspects of the room from their different points of view
Different parts of their bodies	Different parts of their bodies	Different parts of their bodies

It had to be his place of course, she still lived with her parents.

(Afterwards…)

The room	The room	The room
The room	The room	The room

LEENA. You asked why I like you.

GEORGE. *(In Chinese.)* Just joking. 我只是开玩笑。
(wǒ zhǐ shì kāi wán xiào.)

LEENA. But you really don't know?

GEORGE. Okay. Why do you like me?

LEENA. It's because… I'm not telling you.

GEORGE. *(In Chinese.)* Tease. 切。
(qie.)

LEENA. I'm not going to make some list of things.

GEORGE. To keep me on my toes?

LEENA. If you can't see the goodness in you, then…

GEORGE. I am pretty good. But…you are not *(In Chinese.)* turned off? 扫兴?
(sǎo xìng.)

(In English.) By this apartment?

LEENA. It's a scholar's apartment. Wittgenstein in Chinese – impressive!

GEORGE. I like his way of thinking.

LEENA. How so?

GEORGE. It is like the… *(In Chinese.)* connective tissue.
结缔组织。

(jié dì zǔ zhī.)

>   (**LEENA** *doesn't understand, gives a confused
>   look.*)

(In Chinese.) Makes me feel…connected. To new places.
让我们感到连结，到新的地方。

(ràng wǒ men gǎn dào lián jié, dào xīn de dì fang.)

(In English.) Understand?

LEENA. *(Stares at him with a humorous "stupid" look.)* Ni
hao ma?

>   *(They laugh. A beat.)*

So why do you like me?

GEORGE. I could list reasons, but…

LEENA. Don't copy me.

GEORGE. Because you're a Goddess.

>   (**LEENA** *scoffs.*)

Because you treat me well.

LEENA. I treat you well because you treat me well.

GEORGE. Is it that easy?

HENRY. When I say she was the elite, I mean: *she was
the elite.* As daughter of a shipping magnate, she was
courted by everyone, even the heirs of the whitest old
money families, and this was 1970s so interracial dating
was still, well, foreign. And yet she chose my father.
And her father, my grandfather, did not approve.

LEENA (OLDER). *(To* **HENRY** *and* **JESS**.*)* It was rough going during our courtship. My father made things unbearable. And your father let it get to his head. There was always tension. That burst forth without warning. One evening, at his apartment, a wine glass slipped from his hand.

(Video of glass dropping.)

GEORGE. Damnit!

LEENA (OLDER). His reaction was too forceful. It alarmed me.

*(****LEENA**** starts cleaning it up.)*

GEORGE. *(In Chinese.)* No, no I'll do it. 不用，我来就好。 (bú yòng wǒ lái jiù hǎo.)

LEENA. Let me help.

(She insists. He tries to help but soon is just watching.)

Can you help me open the... (garbage).

(He does.)

GEORGE. *(In Chinese.)* Can't believe I did that. 我竟然把它摔碎了。

(wǒ jìng rán bǎ tā shuāi sùi le.)

LEENA. It's just a glass.

GEORGE. I only have two wine glasses.

LEENA. So we'll drink wine out of mugs.

(Beat.)

What.

GEORGE. I cannot think like that.

LEENA. Like what?

GEORGE. Like we can settle for less.

LEENA. That's not what I meant.

> (**GEORGE** *suddenly breaks down. Has to sit down? Deep breathing?*)

What's wrong??

GEORGE. What is wrong is I am not good enough for you.

LEENA. I get to decide what's good for me.

GEORGE. But it is not just about you. It is me. What I need to be. *(In Chinese.)* You do not understand. 你不明白。 (nǐ bù míng bái.)

LEENA. You're thinking like my father. You're letting *him* tell you who you need to be.

GEORGE. This is not about your father *or* you. It's me, okay? *Me. I* need to know that I can take care of you on my own!

LEENA. And I'm *telling you how* to take care of me!!

LEENA (OLDER). It was soon after this that he left me.

HENRY. What?? I didn't know he left you!

LEENA (OLDER). For three whole years. I was devastated. Then one day, three years later, there he is, knocking at our door, dressed to the nines, announcing he's started his own business and wants my hand in marriage. He says this right in front of my parents. My father stands up, stares him up and down, then says: "You think you can fool me? You're the same person you always were. Get out of my sight." I left home to be with George. *(To* **JESS.***)* Father would have approved of *you* though, you're a total class act.

JESS. Well thank you. And I have to say: I know it was tough, but...it sounds pretty romantic. He worked so hard to get you back.

LEENA (OLDER). He wanted to please me so badly. Especially...that first night we spent together.

(The flickering images of sex again.)

Close-ups of aspects of the room from their different points of view	Close-ups of aspects of the room from their different points of view	Close-ups of aspects of the room from their different points of view
Different parts of their bodies	Different parts of their bodies	Different parts of their bodies

LEENA (OLDER). He was very slow. Very thoughtful. He started by taking my –

HENRY. *(To* **LEENA***.)* Okay! Okay! *(To audience.)* I stopped her there. But I knew... I knew she remembered every detail.

Longer sequences of body parts. Clearer and in focus now. A sequence indicating sex	Longer sequences of body parts. Clearer and in focus now. A sequence indicating sex	Longer sequences of body parts. Clearer and in focus now. A sequence indicating sex
Longer sequences of body parts. Clearer and in focus now. A sequence indicating sex	Longer sequences of body parts. Clearer and in focus now. A sequence indicating sex	Longer sequences of body parts. Clearer and in focus now. A sequence indicating sex

LEENA (OLDER). Hint of concrete beneath the tapestries and rug. The hint of dampness. Hint of mothballs that smell like home. Muffled sounds of other tenants. Light under the doorway. Sounds of stoves and fire, and with that the smells of cooking. He apologized for the place but it was paradise to me. But our thoughts turned away from the environment around us. We made our own world. Piece by piece. Second...by second...touch by touch.

(Video out.)

Sorry I was in another place.

JESS. It's okay.

LEENA (OLDER). I just get down sometimes.

*(***JESS** *or* **HENRY** *puts a hand on her.)*

I'll be fine.

HENRY. Do you want us to stay? Or go.

LEENA (OLDER). I'll be alone now.

Jess

Video of car ride *(different details)*	Video of car ride *(different details)*	Video of car ride *(different details)*
Video of car ride *(different details)*	Video of car ride *(different details)*	Video of car ride *(different details)*

HENRY. I remember the ride home after that evening at my mother's. I remember thinking about the memories Jess and *I* made.

Picture of a fun time as a couple, taken by Henry	Picture of a fun time as a couple, taken by Henry	Picture of a fun time as a couple, taken by Henry
Picture of a fun time as a couple, taken by Henry	Picture of a fun time as a couple, taken by Henry	Picture of a fun time as a couple, taken by Henry

I remember looking over at her.

(He does, then looks back out at the audience.)

(To audience.) A feeling of gratitude washes over me at that moment. To be here, in this little hovel of a car, moving through these dark streets with the woman who – who is my home, she really is.

(He looks back at her. Looks back out to audience.)

Of course we've had issues, like every couple. I've been immature at times. Not too long ago I might have asked oooone too many questions about a male co-worker she's close with. I get stupid sometimes. But we talk things through, it's a process.

(He looks back at her. Looks back out to audience.)

Negotiating that sacred little space where our experiences cross paths. And to really be okay when suddenly...she's a mystery. And I can't know her. *(Looking at her.)* Like now. Where is her mind when she gets that faraway look?

JESS. Is In-N-Out still open? Think I'm still hungry.

HENRY. Daly City?

> *(She nods vigorously.)*

Think so. Wanna go?

> *(She smiles a big smile: "Yes." They drive in silence for a beat.)*

JESS. Are you sure it's okay we just left her? Your mother?

HENRY. She likes her privacy.

JESS. Mm.

> *(Silence.)*

And so your grandparents – her parents – still after all that time...

HENRY. They never made amends. It was *her* doing actually.

JESS. What was.

HENRY. She disowned *them.*

JESS. Really.

HENRY. Because her father never gave *my* father the respect she felt he deserved. So she cut them off.

JESS. Wow. She's big on respect.

HENRY. For the people she loves, yes.

Pat's House

HENRY. Thinking back to that car ride, a new angle to my suicide theory started to emerge. Respect. My mom demanded it for her loved ones. But did that extend to after death? What if she tried to *hide* my father's shameful deed when she discovered it? To help him save face? "He was in despair. I tried to help him."

...his death.	*He was in*	*despair.*
I tried	*to help him*	.

I	*tried*	*to*
help	*him*	.

Because if he did...take his own life, with a gun... *where was the gun?* That was the missing part of my theory. There was no gun at the scene, so suicide meant someone had to clean up after him, make it *look* like a random burglary, and take away the gun. And I know, it sounds out there, but – okay, remember I told you I was at a friend's house after school the day my dad died? It was more his mom Pat was my *mom*'s good friend. They were like sisters. And there are details of being at her house that day I can still remember so clearly.

(The images below come up and cycle through as **HENRY** *describes them.)*

Details of Pat's house	Grilled cheese	*Batman: the Animated Series**

---

*A license to produce *The Headlands* does not include a license to publicly display any third-party or copyrighted images. Licensees must acquire rights for any copyrighted images or create their own. For further information, please see the Music and Third Party Materials Use Note on page iii.

Exterior of Pat's house	*Batman: the Animated Series*[*]	Martin playing Game Boy

Like I remember grilled cheese, my favorite. I remember the TV on, and Martin, her son, on the couch playing a Game Boy. In hindsight the whole thing seemed strange because TV, grilled cheese, and Game Boys were all rarities there. And then there's *Batman: the Animated Series*. I never missed an episode. And here's the thing: On days I went to Pat's house after school, my mother *always* picked me up at 3:30, so I'd be back home by 4 when the show started. What I'm saying is I'd never watched *Batman* at another person's house before, so when 4 o'clock came and the opening credits started and still no word from mom, I knew something was wrong. Later I discovered that my mother's 911 call, when she supposedly found the body, was placed at 4:21, but she should have been done teaching by 3, and been on her way to get me. So why did she go home first? What was she doing in the unaccounted for time? *Could she have been cleaning up my father's act?*

Batman[*]	*Batman*[*]	*Batman*[*]
Batman[*]	*Batman*[*]	*Batman*[*]

I needed to make sure I got these details right – the timing, her alibi – so I decided to try and see the case file again.

---

[*] For further information, please see footnote on page 43.

Detective

Details of a police station	Details of a police station	Details of a police station
Details of a police station	Details of a police station	Details of a police station

DETECTIVE. You know, we did a thorough investigation. I looked at every possible angle myself.

HENRY. And this isn't about correcting your investigation.

DETECTIVE. Well it could seem like that, just letting you know.

HENRY. Oh okay.

DETECTIVE. People come in here, requesting case files, thinking we forgot / something.

HENRY. Oh but –

DETECTIVE. But we're trained professionals, you know?

HENRY. Uh huh, yeah.

DETECTIVE. So it's almost like – we can't do our job?

HENRY. I don't mean any offense.

DETECTIVE. Well, it's a little offensive, / just gotta be… honest.

HENRY. Okay, okay.

(Awkward pause.)

DETECTIVE. But I guess anyone can be a detective these days, the whole gig economy, that stuff.

*(A beat. **HENRY** doesn't understand.)*

HENRY. Uh, look, I know you get a lot of requests. But this is my father, and I just…want to look at the case file.

DETECTIVE. Can I give you some advice?

HENRY. Okay.

DETECTIVE. Move on.

HENRY. Excuse me?

DETECTIVE. Because you haven't moved on. Right? Even after all these years? I'm telling you, this won't help you find resolution. You're trying to piece together a puzzle that's not actually a – a – ... *(Getting lost in his own metaphor.)* uh...you know, a *puzzle*. A *complete* puzzle.

HENRY. Nevertheless...

DETECTIVE. When I had my child, do you know what I did? When he was just a baby, every night before he went to bed, I'd imagine, just briefly, that he stopped breathing, and that I held his lifeless body in my arms. I'd imagine my worst fear, my little baby's death, so that when I woke up the next morning, it would feel like...a miracle! A miracle that he was still alive!

(**HENRY** *doesn't know how to respond.*)

What I'm saying is that I'd be so grateful and so humbled by this extra day with him. This puts things in perspective, it's a technique of the Stoics. When each of my parents fell ill, I did the same with them: every day I'd imagine them dead, so when they actually died, the blow wasn't that bad. So what I'm saying is...if you imagined his death beforehand, you wouldn't have this problem.

HENRY. I have no idea what you're talking about, what problem.

DETECTIVE. *(Leans in.)* Well, the problem of death. Right? You're searching for answers you don't even have the questions for.

HENRY. *(To audience.)* There's something to what he said.

DETECTIVE. Okay. One case file coming up. Just so you don't think we're hiding anything.

> *(He shambles off.* **JESS** *enters, a little out of breath, but very upbeat.)*

JESS. Hey!

HENRY. Hey!

> *(They embrace.)*

JESS. Sorry I'm late.

HENRY. No problem.

JESS. Did you talk to anyone yet?

HENRY. Yeah, he's going to get me the case file.

JESS. Oh yeah?? Just like that?

HENRY. Well – we'll see. *(In a bit of a whisper.)* It's – the actual guy.

JESS. What guy.

HENRY. The detective from my father's case.

JESS. From all that time ago?

HENRY. Yeah, that's who I'm talking to.

JESS. Oh wow. He's still here?

HENRY. Hey do you need some water? Should we try and / find a –

JESS. Oh no, I'm okay. Sorry again for being / late, bus problems.

> *(**HENRY** brushes it off at " / .")*

This is kind of exciting. I mean *you've* done this / before, but –

HENRY. What.

JESS. Like a *field* investigation, at a station.

HENRY. Oh! Yeah. It's hit or miss sometimes but...

> *(Slight beat as they wait. She's still a little out of breath.)*

You sure you don't want any water, / or –

JESS. *(Looking around.)* Actually yeah, I wonder if there's – ...

> *(**DETECTIVE** returns with case file.)*

DETECTIVE. Okay, here you go. *(Noticing **JESS**.)*. Oh, hello!

JESS. Hi, I'm Jess.

DETECTIVE. Hello Jess.

HENRY. This is my girlfriend. Is it okay if she – ...

DETECTIVE. Sure, let's get a whole team in here to check my work! *(To **JESS**.)* I'm kidding. I'm very secure.

> *(Slight awkward beat. **HENRY** begins to flip through the folder.)*

JESS. So you were the actual investigator on this case.

DETECTIVE. Yup. I was the guy who didn't find the guy. Which is why we need these task rabbits now, right?

> *(A beat. They don't understand.)*

JESS. Uhh, yes!

> *(Light laughter from all.)*

So let me ask you: did you have any other, like...pet theories?

DETECTIVE. My theory is that there were a number of unsolved break-ins at the time.

JESS. Even though this one didn't fit the pattern.

DETECTIVE. We're looking for the most likely scenario.

HENRY. Did you question my mother?

DETECTIVE. Of course.

HENRY. I mean at length.

DETECTIVE. What do you mean.

HENRY. Like her timeline, alibi...

DETECTIVE. Whoa. Hold on. *(Does a disbelieving laugh.)* You telling me you suspect your *mother*? Boy / that's some –

HENRY. No, I didn't say that.

DETECTIVE. That's some Greek shit right there. Not like current Greeks, I'm not a / racist, or –

JESS. No, what we –

DETECTIVE. But you actually believe *she* is the / ...

JESS. No, not the *culprit*, but we're... Should I – *(Turns to* HENRY *for permission to continue. He nods.)* We're working on a theory that she could have helped, uh... clean up after a – an *intentional* act.

DETECTIVE. *Suicide*? Really?? God, that's – *(Does a disbelieving laugh.)* didn't know you were going *there*. Jesus.

JESS. There were no other suspects?

DETECTIVE. Only his father's employee.

HENRY. Paul Cheung.

DETECTIVE. Yeah. But he had a solid alibi.

HENRY. And you suspected him because of his criminal record.

DETECTIVE. No. Because of the video.

HENRY. Video? What video?

DETECTIVE. You didn't know about the video?

HENRY. What video??

DETECTIVE. Wow, you guys are probably gonna make a really big deal out of this then. Neighbor's surveillance video. Only photos now. And it's from the other end of the block, so doesn't show your door or anything. The timing matches. But it's probably just a passerby. His face is blurred, but he sort of resembled Paul. *(Preemptively defensive.) Yes because he's Chinese but I asked some Chinese colleagues and they said it could be him too.*

HENRY. *(Out of the scene.)* It was blurry, but I could see his face. It wasn't Paul. I felt my blood run cold. I recognized the man.

The surveillance image of the man	The surveillance image of the man	The surveillance image of the man
The surveillance image of the man	The surveillance image of the man	The surveillance image of the man

Tom

(With these next few scenes, the play takes on a distinctly darker, more sinister atmosphere.)

The surveillance image of the man	The surveillance image of the man	EMDR
EMDR	The surveillance image of the man	The surveillance image of the man

HENRY. *(Looking at the surveillance image.)* It's one of those things where, when you're a child and you encounter something that doesn't seem quite right, you instinctively don't pursue it, for fear of what the truth might be. Well, this man, at one point, appeared in my house, and it didn't seem right so I pushed it down. All these years. But this photograph brought it back.

Detail of living room	Detail of living room	Detail of living room
Detail of living room	Detail of living room	Detail of living room

The doorbell rings one day. My mother's home but my father's out. She opens the door, and I see him beyond. At first I think he's a stranger, but then they start talking in whispers. Until my mother relents with...

LEENA. Okay, okay.

HENRY. He enters. Again. Doesn't feel right. They're in the living room and she's serving him tea. I'm watching through a door crack, then build up the courage to venture in.

LEENA. Oh! Henry this is Tom.

TOM. Hello. Nice to meet you. You're a good looking boy.

HENRY. She flashes him a look. Can't tell what it means. "Who are you?" I boldly ask.

TOM. I'm a friend.

LEENA. He used to be my piano student, but now he's our friend.

HENRY. I want to ask if by "our" she means "dad too."

LEENA. Henry, go to your room for a bit. Tom was just telling me something personal, so we need some privacy.

HENRY. I don't move. I want to put myself in the middle of this, whatever it is.

LEENA. Go on, and we'll go get pizza afterwards.

HENRY. *(To audience.)* Okay. Fine.

> *(An atmosphere shift to something a little more surreal.* **HENRY** *moves away from the scene.* **TOM** *makes sure he's gone, then rises and embraces* **LEENA.** *She resists a bit but is into it.)*

LEENA. *(Not completely saying no.)* No, don't.

TOM. He's a good looking kid.

LEENA. You shouldn't have talked to him.

TOM. He'll be fine.

LEENA. I know, but...

TOM. I'm sorry for coming. But not too sorry.

> *(They kiss.)*

LEENA. I like spontaneity, but—

TOM. I didn't know he was home sick today.

LEENA. I know, so just...

(Gently pushing him out the door...)

TOM. When can we...

LEENA. I'll call you.

(One last kiss.)

HENRY. I extrapolated that last part. That last part I didn't see, but it's a truth I pushed down. Children know things. And with this memory recalled, other memories start to bloom.

The Window

(The same "window" video setup from earlier in the play. **GEORGE** *is in the same position, looking out the window.)*

Aspects of living room	Living room window, open	Aspects of living room
Aspects of living room	Closer view of the night street	Aspects of living room

HENRY. Remember that scene at the window I described earlier? Well, I suddenly remember the *complete* version. *(To* **GEORGE.***)* Why are you looking out the window?

GEORGE. *(Looking out.)* It's nice sometimes to look out and not in.

(He looks at **HENRY.***)*

(Smiling.) Or you can get trapped in your own brain. Do you know what I mean by that?

HENRY. Uhhh...

(Slight beat.)

GEORGE. Your dad's just being weird.

HENRY. I'd forgotten what happened next. I had *pressed* him. *(To* **GEORGE.***)* What are you really looking at?

*(**GEORGE** looks at him.)*

GEORGE. I'm looking at... I'm looking at your mother.

HENRY. Where is she?

GEORGE. In her car. Down the street.

HENRY. *(To audience.)* I peeked out but couldn't see. I knew I wasn't supposed to ask this, but – *(To* **GEORGE.***)* Can I go to her?

GEORGE. No.

HENRY. I want to go to her.

GEORGE. You can't.

HENRY. Why?

>*(Pause.)*

GEORGE. She's talking to a friend.

HENRY. I knew it was him. Mom didn't come in until much later. They barely spoke. There was a chill.

>*(Beat.)*

Things we know in our gut but push down. My mother had an affair.

George and Leena

(Video and staging: Suggestion of the Dinner Scene but possibly deconstructed.)

HENRY. And it all starts clicking into place.

Kitchen wall. Flickering?	Blank	Blank
Blank	Blank	Kitchen wall. Flickering?

LEENA. I just wish uh...

GEORGE. There was something more you could do. There's nothing. Nothing can repair what you've done.

HENRY. It *wasn't* a perfect marriage.

LEENA. I want us to be a team. Like always.

GEORGE. We're not a team anymore.

HENRY. Their tripwires set from the very beginning.

(Suddenly: Video and staging add in – or replace with – suggestion of George's tenement apt., the argument scene. Video: The glass falling.)

GEORGE. Damnit!!

(Video of the glass falling repeating on a loop.)

Glass falling	George's tenement room	George's tenement room
George's tenement room	Glass falling	Glass falling

I am not good enough for you.

HENRY. Insecurities, from the beginning.

LEENA. You're thinking like my father. You're letting *him* tell you who you need to be.

HENRY. Inadequacies. Always pulling him back into his own head.

GEORGE. It's me, okay? *Me. I* need to know that I can take care of you on my own!

HENRY. He was driven, always on a mission that never ended.

LEENA. And I'm *telling you how* to take care of me!!

HENRY. He left her because he was on a quest for *himself.* He neglects her. He has the capacity to neglect her.

GEORGE. I am not good enough for you.

HENRY. His leaving. Their signature trauma, carried over all these years.

Marin Headlands hike	View to Land's End	Glass falling
Glass falling	View to Land's End	Lucca's Delicatessen

GEORGE. I like looking at it from here, from far away, because it's a special place, but it's changed.

> (*During the following, video cycles through a single image – but possibly repeated on several panels – which represents each part of what* **HENRY***'s talking about. Perhaps it could be three panels with a single image, that is staggered when a new image comes up. For example...*)

Marin Headlands hike	Marin Headlands hike	Tom
Marin Headlands Hike	Tom	Tom

Walter	Walter	Tom
Walter	Tom	Tom

Tom	Tom	George at window
Tom	George at window	George at window

HENRY. He's trying too hard to craft a moment. There was always some tension in those hikes, if I'm honest. He's always carried tension. So: insecurities, baggage, neglect. She flirts at a piano lesson with someone not so *burdened*. Dad picks up on her distance, gets *more* insecure as a result. Looks to their bank account for validation and it's not enough, needs more to match her father so he takes more, gets caught, and then... Then what... He's caught, family's in trouble, play time's over with the new man because family comes first so she breaks it off, in the car, while my dad watches from the window. Breaks it off but the man, *he* doesn't like it, he's not well – I sensed that when I met him in our house, he seemed unstable – he gets angry – wants my father out of the way because he's obsessed with her – comes to the house, and – and – ...

Tom aiming gun	Tom aiming gun	Tom aiming gun
Tom aiming gun	Tom aiming gun	Tom aiming gun

EMDR	EMDR	EMDR
EMDR	EMDR	EMDR

(We hear the chords from earlier.)

Leena's left hand on keyboard	Leena's eyes	Leena's right hand at keyboard
George's left hand on keyboard	George's eyes	George's right hand on keyboard

HENRY. Those chords, those mysterious chords Dad
played, right before his death. I remember now. It was
her composition, not his. He played it when she was
gone. Gone to that other man. Like a bird sending a
special song through the forest to its lost mate. He was
trying to call her back.

> *(Music reaches a final conclusion, a final
> chord.)*

Jess

>*(Suddenly all video freezes. Slightly staticky in silence. Sound of a key in the lock. Door opening.)*

HENRY. Honey?

>*(No response.)*

Honey... Jess?

JESS. *(Offstage still.)* Yes, just a minute.

HENRY. *(To audience.)* Something's off.

>*(A pause. Then **JESS** slowly enters but stops in the doorway. All video out. A sudden, unexpected "natural" look. A pause in this new environment, with **JESS** in the doorway. **JESS** has a totally different energy from before. Where before she was energized, matching **HENRY**'s infectious energy, now there's something more "naturalistic" to the acting. Like documentary realism. The following is played as gentle and loving as possible. Push against the anger. Make the beats, pauses and silences pregnant, even if they feel uncomfortably long.)*

Hey... What's up?

>*(She doesn't immediately respond.)*

Is everything okay? What's – (going on)...

JESS. Listen uh... I have something I need to say.

HENRY. *(Nervous.)* Okay...

>*(Pause. It's hard for her to continue.)*

What is it – / just – just –

JESS. Wait. Just let me – ...

> *(He gives her the floor. She takes a deep breath.)*

I've decided I need to get away for a little bit.

HENRY. Um... Get away?

JESS. For about a week. Or more. Just to my sister's.

> *(**HENRY** waits for her to continue but she doesn't for a beat.)*

HENRY. Are you breaking up with me??

JESS. No. I'm not.

HENRY. Oh thank god.

JESS. I just think that...with this case you're doing... I've decided I *do* need some distance from it. Like we talked about. So...

> *(**HENRY** takes a moment to absorb this, but is still confused.)*

HENRY. Sorry, talked about? What do you mean?

JESS. What do you mean what do I mean?

> *(They both have a beat of mutual confusion.)*

What we talked about in couples counseling. My needing to set boundaries for myself, that whole talk.

HENRY. Oh right.

JESS. And how a break for me was an option.

HENRY. But I didn't think that was serious.

JESS. What??

HENRY. Just the break part.

JESS. Of course it was serious.

HENRY. Oh yeah no of course. Of course.

   (A silence.)

Um. I'm sorry but I'm still just having a little bit of – ... Because weren't we *just* at the police station and you were really *excited* about the case?

JESS. *(Confused, troubled.)* Henry, you thought I was excited?

   (**HENRY** *is genuinely taken aback for a beat.*)

HENRY. Am I missing something here?

JESS. It was an inconvenience. I was at a business lunch and you pulled me away because you said it was really important but you hadn't even *found* anything yet, when I arrived. It was a big inconvenience to me, and the fact you can't see that is –

   (She stops herself before she gets too angry.)

And then I just got this crazy idea that...maybe you thought I was having lunch with *Mark*, and *that's* why you pulled me / away to –

HENRY. No! That's absolutely / not what I –

JESS. Okay. Okay. But the fact that I *thought* that – it's – That's why I need this distance. I can't think like this. I can't get pulled in.

HENRY. What do you mean pulled in?

   (Pause.)

JESS. You were *severely* depressed over your mother's death. You were. But instead of *dealing* with that, you started saying your *father* was depressed. Then I get this text from you saying your mother had an affair, and *we* had just had that fight about *Mark*. And – and so you're not thinking straight. You're not seeing clearly. *(A little shaky.)* And it's affecting me, and it's not healthy for me.

(A silence.)

HENRY. I don't want you to go. I'm sorry.

JESS. It's best for both of us. You need space to grieve, for both of your parents, on your own.

(Beat.)

HENRY. Are you saying I should drop the case?

JESS. That's not what I'm saying at all.

HENRY. Will you stay if I drop it?

JESS. That's not how this works.

(Pause.)

HENRY. *(To audience.)* She assures me once again this isn't a break-up. She packs a suitcase in silence and leaves.

(The play rests in an inconclusive silence for a beat. The following is delivered with more resignation that before, an ambiguousness.)

If...

(Slight beat.)

If...

(Slight beat.)

If there was one person who could confirm my mother's affair, it was her oldest friend in the world: Pat. I decide to pay her a visit.

Pat

Details of Pat's house	Pat's living room	Details of Pat's house
Exterior of Pat's house	Pat's living room	*Batman: The Animated Series**

PAT. Something's up with you. I can tell.

HENRY. Huh?

PAT. Something just happened to you. What's wrong.

HENRY. Nothing happened. I'm fine.

(She looks at him dubiously, does a little grunt re: she doesn't believe him.)

Maybe just missing my mother.

(She studies him, still not believing.)

PAT. As you should.

HENRY. I know she was like a sister to you.

PAT. That she was. Do you want some tea?

HENRY. Oh no, I'm fine.

PAT. Oh you're not staying long?

HENRY. Oh uh sure okay.

PAT. You don't *have* to stay long, if you have somewhere to be.

HENRY. Oh no, I want to stay.

PAT. I mean you came *here*. I'm not putting a / gun to your head.

HENRY. I know, I know. Thank you.

PAT. Okay. I'll get some tea.

---

* For further information, please see footnote on page 43.

(She prepares tea. The following might be played with her in another room, and/or with her periodically coming back in while she prepares the tea.)

HENRY. Since you were like sisters, I suppose you shared things with each other. Like sisters do.

PAT. Like what.

HENRY. Like secrets, things like that.

(Beat.)

PAT. What are you up to.

(Beat.)

HENRY. What were mom and dad like. As husband and wife.

PAT. They were wonderful as husband and wife. Why.

HENRY. Always?

PAT. What?

HENRY. They were always wonderful together?

(Beat.)

PAT. I don't like this.

HENRY. What.

PAT. This – *energy* you're giving off.

HENRY. Oh! / I'm –

PAT. This – this relentless, masculine energy.

HENRY. I'm sorry, I didn't – I can leave.

PAT. But I'm making tea.

HENRY. Okay, I'm staying. I'm just curious these days. I'm sorry.

PAT. I'll forgive you. Because I see your mother in you.

> *(She goes and gets the tea and brings it in. Pause.)*

They had their ups and downs. But the real problems were all in the beginning. I've known your mother a long time, I was there from the beginning.

HENRY. What problems from the beginning? Only if you want to...

PAT. Only if I want to what?

HENRY. Tell me.

PAT. *You* want to know, right?

HENRY. Yes, you're / right.

PAT. *(Muttering.)* Just say what you want.

HENRY. *I* want to know. Please tell me.

> *(Slight beat.)*

PAT. Well, the first years were rough because of your grandfather's disapproval of your father. They even split up for a time.

HENRY. Yeah she told me about that.

PAT. But they found their way back to each other. Why don't you tell me what are you're *really* after.

> *(Pause.)*

HENRY. Okay. I'm not saying this from any place of judgment toward my mother. But I remember there was a – ...a man. To whom she seemed close, when I was a child.

> *(**PAT** stares coldly at him for a beat.)*

I was wondering, if you knew him – ... It's this man.

*(He hands her printout of the surveillance footage. **PAT** reacts with recognition. Stares at it a long time. Then looks away from picture and **HENRY**.)*

Again. No anger.

(Pause.)

PAT. I knew your mother well. She entrusted me with her secrets.

HENRY. I love my mother. I know things get complicated.

PAT. Yes, complicated. This wasn't your mother's lover. Which I know is what you're thinking. Your mother would never do anything like that.

(Beat.)

This man is your brother.

(Video goes haywire. A chaotic mix of many images that have come before, but always with the EMDR pendulum swinging underneath.)

Chaotic mixture of images from throughout the play	Chaotic mixture of images from throughout the play	Chaotic mixture of images from throughout the play
EMDR pendulum	EMDR pendulum	EMDR pendulum

It happened early on. That was the real reason they broke up.

Video of the glass falling	Video of the glass falling	*Batman*[*], then other things

---

[*] For further information, please see footnote on page 43.

EMDR pendulum	EMDR pendulum	EMDR pendulum

When they were young romantic souls running around San Francisco, they got pregnant, with him, your brother.

Chinatown tenement house	Images from the sex sequence	Images from the sex sequence
EMDR pendulum	EMDR pendulum	EMDR pendulum

Your grandfather said, "no," your father wasn't going to raise this kid. He wasn't a suitable man. And your father, to your mother's horror, agreed! Agreed he wasn't good enough! Your father lacked…independence of mind. Even though he played the rebel. So the decision was made that the child would be given up. The decision was made *for* your mother – by her father, and your father too.

HENRY. That's when he left?

PAT. He was banned from seeing her during her pregnancy.

HENRY. By Grandpa.

PAT. And her too. She was wounded. Because he didn't fight for her. And their son. She didn't want to see him.

HENRY. But she took him back. Eventually.

(**PAT** *shrugs.*)

PAT. Guess they loved each other. Stranger things have happened.

HENRY. And the boy…

PAT. They lost track of him. And when they started over, they agreed to have a blank slate. That meant no more mention of him. But…

HENRY. He came back.

PAT. Turns out he was close by the whole time. Living just North of here, in Marin, in San Rafael. He had done some digging and found them. He met your mother first. Then, she had a talk with George.

(Video now might be hazy to reflect the memory filters it's being passed through. Same setup as the "dinner scene.")

Kitchen wall	Window showing nighttime outside	Kitchen wall
Blank	Blank	Blank

GEORGE. What's he like?

LEENA. He's a very nice man.

GEORGE. And he's – how old is he?

LEENA. Around seventeen.

GEORGE. And what does he do? What's / his...

LEENA. Odd jobs. Cleans pools. Fix-it things.

GEORGE. And he lived up in Marin this whole time?

(Pause.)

LEENA. I want you to meet him.

GEORGE. I still wish you didn't let him into our house without talking with me.

LEENA. Did you hear what I said?

(Pause.)

GEORGE. We just need to be very careful about...not sending any kind of message to him.

LEENA. He just wanted to meet us.

GEORGE. You said it seemed like he needed *family*.

LEENA. Well is that *so terrible*?

GEORGE. Well, we need to think about Henry, how this would affect him, if / suddenly –

LEENA. Yeah but –

GEORGE. So that's – that's our top priority. Our family *right here*. It's going to be a very big deal, if we start to…

> (*He doesn't know how to finish, perhaps does an exasperated laugh.*)

LEENA. You owe him a *meeting*.

> (*Pause.*)

I dream about him.

> (*Pause.*)

GEORGE. Okay. I'll meet him. But we can't promise him anything. We can't give him what he needs.

> (**LEENA** *shakes her head.*)

LEENA. I just wish uh…

GEORGE. There was something more you could do.

> (*He waits while* **LEENA** *somehow indicates the affirmative.*)

LEENA. I want us to be a team on this. Like always.

> (**GEORGE** *doesn't respond.*)

You're just…acting very different now.

GEORGE. I'm sorry.

LEENA. It's just…very hard.

(Her attention is perked up by **HENRY** *in the doorway – not necessarily the physical actor.)*

(In a quick whisper, to **GEORGE**.*)* Henry.

*(***GEORGE** *springs up and moves toward wherever the child is indicated.)*

GEORGE. Okay buddy, come on, it's time to go to bed.

(Back to video of Pat's house.)

HENRY. Do you know where to find him?

PAT. I know where he works. He's still up North.

(Slight beat.)

Take care of yourself.

HENRY. I will.

PAT. No really. I can see that…you're suffering. Take care of it.

San Rafael

Video of drive to Marin, across the Golden Gate Bridge	Video of drive to Marin, across the Golden Gate Bridge	Video of drive to Marin, across the Golden Gate Bridge
Video of drive to Marin, across the Golden Gate Bridge	Video of drive to Marin, across the Golden Gate Bridge	Video of drive to Marin, across the Golden Gate Bridge

(**HENRY** *drives in silence for a good while, the shock of the previous scene still with him.*)

HENRY. I'm driving. Driving. Driving to the brother I never knew I had.

(*Pause.*)

Driving. To confront the man who might have killed my – *our* father. Driving but... I don't even have a plan. What will I do when I meet him? I can't believe I have no plan.

(*Pause.*)

I follow the paces of Google Maps, drive into the Canal area of San Rafael where Pat told me he worked. A tackle shop near the Bay. I park a distance away and watch. There he is. He emerges.

Details of the area	Details of the area	Details of the area
Details of the area	Details of the area	Details of the area

(**TOM** *emerges, smokes.*)

He looks weather-beaten. Hardened. Looking at his face, I see my father. And my mother. And myself. I stay in my car, paralyzed.

(Pause.)

I think about Jess. How she kept saying I'm seeing things through a certain lens.

(Pause.)

I wait 'til sundown when I see my brother finally drive off. I follow him to his house, then knock on his door.

Tom

*(At this point in time the entire play suddenly and joltingly changes perspectives. The video screens reflect this change by taking on a totally new quality we've never seen before. We are no longer in **HENRY**'s headspace now, but **TOM**'s. Everything that follows is now from **TOM**'s point of view.)*

Blank	Blank	Blank
Blank	Blank	Blank

TOM. And there he stands. Henry. Of course, I know who he is. I've kept tabs on him all this time, after all. Observed him from a distance for so long he feels like… well, like a long-lost brother. I invite him inside. He steps in. He seems a bit nervous and rambles a bit at first…

HENRY. There are so many ways to make an introduction. And I'm not sure what the *best* way is, so I'm just gonna jump right in. Okay?

TOM. I tell him to have a seat. He does, and then…he talks. And talks and talks. And it all comes out. The entire journey he took to get here. He tells it in such vivid detail that I can see it all play out in my mind's eye.

(We see a video of the entire show up until now – the stage show, with video etc. – in super fast speed, spread across all screens.)

The entire show	The entire show	The entire show
The entire show	The entire show	The entire show

Every instance. Every memory. Every memory of someone else's memory, it's all so vivid. I can see it. He's a good storyteller. But when I hear how rich, how detailed his own memories are, and how the good ones, the ones with father and mother, how they – I can see this – how *they* create the foundation from which he travels forth in life, how *those memories* are his engine...

The entire show	Nostalgic video images used before	The entire show
The entire show	Nostalgic video images used before	The entire show

I dunno, it suddenly makes me feel...upset. Because while that's his memory space he's giving me, mine *(Indicating the screens behind him.)* is very different.

(Video shifts to murky images with more dulled, muddy color palates. We can faintly make out disturbing images of parental mistreatment, but the images are not vivid.)

Tom's childhood	Tom's childhood	Tom's childhood
Tom's childhood	Tom's childhood	Tom's childhood

I put them to words. I tell him about *my* life. From the beginning. Well, after I was given up. How I always felt darkness nipping at my heels. How year after year dragged on until every last filament of trust had disappeared. I tell him about that first home I was placed in, the one where that motherfucker hit me, tormented me, and his wife stood silent while he did it. And how I fought back, and because I fought back was labeled "troubled." And how I actually *became* troubled because of that, *became* the tormentor in subsequent placements. (I didn't tell him all of that.) But I did say how I bounced around, family to family, until I came of age and went on my merry way. Then how I got into some trouble with some really bad people and so, not knowing where to turn, I decided to find the only two people who maybe couldn't say no to helping me. I tracked them down. Observed them. (I didn't tell him this either.) But boy did they look happy. All three of them. How that kid was being filled with such great memories. My mother. My mother looked to me to be a saint. I met her outside her workspace and over coffee she said:

LEENA. I've dreamt of you.

TOM. I've dreamt of you too. You seem so close to the person in my dreams.

LEENA. I just want to say I'm sorry.

TOM. You don't need to be sorry.

LEENA. But –

TOM. What's important is that we're meeting now.

LEENA. I have so many questions. What's your life been like?

TOM. It hasn't been easy.

LEENA. I wish you hadn't said that.

TOM. Sorry.

LEENA. No – ... I mean, I wish it wasn't true.

(She smiles at him, takes his hands.)

Hiking with Father

Tom's version of the Headlands trip	Tom's version of the Headlands trip	Tom's version of the Headlands trip
Tom's version of the Headlands trip	Tom's version of the Headlands trip	Tom's version of the Headlands trip

TOM. I tell him about meeting our father. We went to the Marin Headlands. *(To* **GEORGE**.*)* Thanks for coming here with me.

GEORGE. Of course.

TOM. I hope I don't come across as – ... I mean I picked this place because I heard it's where you bring your son. From Mother. *(To audience.)* I of course didn't tell him – or Henry – it was because I'd followed them here before. *(Back to* **GEORGE**.*)* So I just assumed it's a place you liked. But... Does it feel weird to be here? With me?

GEORGE. It's –

TOM. Because I'm not trying to *weirdly* recreate anything, just thought you liked the place, so I suggested it. I'm talking too much now, huh.

GEORGE. It's okay. Don't worry about it.

TOM. But it is really beautiful up here.

(*Silence.*)

GEORGE. So. Leena told me about your situation.

TOM. Oh, god, that's –

GEORGE. It's okay. I don't even want to know how it happened.

TOM. It's just so embarrassing. I knew I shouldn't have gotten involved with these guys, / it's just – ...

GEORGE. It's okay. Seriously. I think that – ... You gotta do what you gotta do. And you, I know you're a sharp, talented young man, and you had to do certain things to survive. And I admire you, for having the strength to survive, to take care of yourself, no matter what it takes. So I want to...help you now. I'm going to give you the money to make things square with these people.

TOM. That's a lot of money.

GEORGE. I've lined it up.

(**TOM** *does a disbelieving laugh.*)

TOM. Wow that's – ... I don't know what to say.

GEORGE. It's something I need to do. For you. Yeah? Okay? We'll find a time for you to come over and pick it up.

(**TOM** *nods. They stand in silence.*)

TOM. You saved my life.

GEORGE. Believe me, it's the least I can do. You need the opportunity to start from scratch. To reach your fullest potential. You have it in you.

TOM. Have what in me?

GEORGE. Great promise.

TOM. How can you tell that, you don't even know me.

GEORGE. Well, I can see it.

(*Silence.*)

TOM. This is really just great. To be able to spend time here with you. To meet you. Finally. Thank you.

(*He goes in for a hug.* **GEORGE** *awkwardly accepts it.*)

I want to uh...spend more time with you. Is that okay? I've gotten to know Mom so well now, and I know you've been busy, but – and even Henry, my own brother! I hope that's okay. Better late than never, right?

(**GEORGE** *smiles but doesn't respond.*)

And I don't – it doesn't have to be all time or anything, just to – to *sometimes* –

(**GEORGE** *nods.*)

Or all the time! I dunno!

(**GEORGE** *stops nodding.*)

I don't want this generous payment to be a…a buy-off.

GEORGE. I wish you didn't say that.

TOM. I'm sorry, I'm so sorry. I don't know what came over me.

GEORGE. Listen, Tom. I'm not sure quite how to say this, but… I have…a very set way of raising a child. And, this means I can't – … I'm now raising Henry in a certain way. I'm sorry that it wasn't you, but –

TOM. I'm not asking you to –

GEORGE. But please, hear me out. I'm just – what I need to do right now is do what's best for Henry. And what that means is he needs a normal – but not normal, but – what he's used to.

TOM. A better / childhood.

GEORGE. No. One that he's used to. And, and so something like this would be…disruptive. And confusing. I mean maybe later on down the line, when he's older – …but right now – I hear what you need, and want, I do – but after this payment, for right now I'll need to give you support from…from afar. In spirit. It's just…

TOM. So no contact. That's what you're saying.

GEORGE. You're a good kid. A strong kid. I'm positive you'll succeed.

The Window

The perspective of the interior of the window, from before	The inside of a car, at night	The exterior of the Wong house at night, with window light on, George's silhouette visible
The inside of a car, at night	The inside of a car, at night	The inside of a car, at night

TOM. *(To audience.)* Soon after meeting father, I went to their house one night, unannounced. I just want to say hi, but mother quickly shuffles me into her car. In her car, as we talk, I can feel George watching us, from the window up above.

> *(We are now inside the car that* **GEORGE** *was watching from the window previously.* **TOM** *sits with* **LEENA**.)*

So you're saying we can't see each other anymore.

LEENA. Just for now. Until we figure things out.

TOM. Did I cause a rift between you two?

LEENA. We had a discussion about spending more time with you. And – ... We're a team. That's how it's always been. So if one of us – ...

TOM. Him, if *he* doesn't want me.

LEENA. It's not / that he –

TOM. I don't care about him anymore. It's you. I just want to spend time with *you*. Is that too much to ask?

LEENA. No, of course not.

TOM. Do you like spending time with me?

LEENA. Yes.

TOM. I can't go back now. Now that I've met you. I can't go back to being alone in the world. Once a week. Can I see you once a week?

LEENA. It's not a bargaining / – …

TOM. Once a month? Please? Can I at least call you?

(**LEENA** *doesn't respond.*)

The light is on. In your house. I think I can see him in the window. He's watching us, huh. I wish you didn't have to listen to him. It's because I'm not good enough.

LEENA. No. I –

TOM. *(To audience.)* I imagine their conversation. I can guess what he said about me.

GEORGE. …I'm saying I met with him, like you wanted me to, and – I just don't like his – his *vibe*. He makes me nervous.

LEENA. His *vibe*?? You're talking about his *vibe*??

GEORGE. And those people he was involved with. What kind of a person is this?

LEENA. This is our son!

GEORGE. Look, I don't think he's *well*. Okay? Like even how he found us. It was like he – he was stalking us!

LEENA. It's not stalking, it's a child trying to find his parents!

GEORGE. I just don't –

LEENA. Maybe he doesn't act right because he's had such a hard life.

GEORGE. We're not responsible for that. Okay? We're *not*.

LEENA. It's wrong to quarantine someone just because the situation's messy. That's what we did in the first place! We gave him up because you and my father were so obsessed with – with this living up to some *idea* of what you *needed to be,* how our life was *supposed to be* – and he didn't *fit* / into the idea, so –

GEORGE. No – I was –

LEENA. You guys were just so *caught,* in both of your heads, in this *obsession* of – of –

GEORGE. I was doing what your father wanted because of *you!* I was doing this for *you!* So we could –

LEENA. How can you say you were doing it for me?!! You weren't seeing what I really wanted!!! *I didn't want to give him up!! You forced me to!!!*

(*Big, pregnant silence.*)

GEORGE. I don't want this man around Henry.

LEENA. He's in despair. And I want to help him.

GEORGE. Which is why I'm going to give him the money. And that's it. No more.

LEENA. So I can't see him anymore. You're forcing me to give him up. Again.

GEORGE. We're a team. Right?

TOM. At least that's how I imagine it. Her standing up for me, my father, well, my father seeing through me. Being a monster for seeing through me. A monster compared to my mother, the angel, because the next thing she said in the car was…

LEENA. Just remember. Even if I don't see you for a long, long time, I have your back. Okay? I'm with you.

TOM. (*To audience.*) Angel.

The Headlands

TOM. As I relay my story to him, I can see the expression on his face changing. Where there was once fear and predation, a cautious empathy now creeps in. By the time I get to the car conversation, I can see he feels compassion. But still... I see he has *some* doubts, so what happens next surprises me. He looks at me long and hard, as if turning over several game plans, then...

> (**HENRY** *puts an arm on* **TOM***'s shoulder. Holds it there, then withdraws.*)

And then he leaves. Without saying another word. Just leaves. What would have happened if he'd pursued things a little further? What would have happened if I'd said I went back to our parents' house some days after that car talk, ostensibly to get the money from father, but that I actually had a different plan, involving the gun I brought along? And what if I told him the plan *wasn't* to shoot our father, but to put the gun to my *own* head and pull the trigger as he watched? What would've happened if I'd said that at the final moment, in the midst of his protests, a spell came over me and, as if guided by an invisible hand, I slowly, in a trance, turned the gun his way instead; and then, in tears, allowed that strange spirit to take my trigger finger and, gentle as a feather, pull it. Just. So.

> (*He acts this out with his finger.*)

And that I called mother right after, in a panic, and she came straight over from her work. What would he have done if I said all this to him?

> (*Slight beat.*)

I'll never know.

> (*Video now pivots away from* **TOM***'s POV into something much more limited than before.*)

Driving on the Golden Gate Bridge, away from Marin	Driving on the Golden Gate Bridge, away from Marin	The Headlands
Driving on the Golden Gate Bridge, away from Marin	The Headlands	Driving on the Golden Gate Bridge, away from Marin

(**HENRY** *driving.*)

HENRY. *(On phone.)* Hi Jess. Look I know I shouldn't be calling you, but... *(She says something kind.)* But still... I want to respect your space. I just really, really wanted to hear your voice right now. *(She says something kind.)* So uh, I *definitely* know you don't want to hear about the case but *(She says something kind, urging him to continue.)* – well – I found him. *(She asks who it is.)* The person I think is... *(She is surprised, asks who.)* My – okay my brother. But – *(She is shocked he has a brother, asks rapid fire questions.)* It's a long story. But the reason I called you is, I wanted to tell you that – ... I'm not going to pursue this anymore. *(She says okay, then: why not?)* Well, I think that uh... Whatever happened...he's...suffered. He's suffered enough.

(He turns his attention to the audience.)

We say we miss each other. We say goodbye. And in the rearview mirror, as I cross the Golden Gate Bridge, I see The Headlands, now dark silhouettes. The place is different now. Across the bridge, where my brother lives, will now be a place of mystery, a place of depths I can't conceive of, swimming in darkness...at a distance. I had some happy memories with my father there, but things change. This would be my new view of The Headlands. This is how they would be. Until they change again.

End of Play